Conga Crocodile

Nicole Rubel

Houghton Mifflin Company   Boston 1993

Library of Congress Cataloging-in-Publication Data

Rubel, Nicole.
  Conga Crocodile / Nicole Rubel.
     p.   cm.
  Summary: Conga Crocodile's talent as a drummer isn't appreciated
by anyone, except his grandmother, until he is recruited by a band
and becomes a star.
   ISBN 0-395-58773-5
   [1. Drum—Fiction.   2. Crocodiles—Fiction.]   I. Title.
PZ7.R828Co   1993   92-31856
[E]—dc20   CIP
                          AC

Printed in the United States of America

BVG   10 9 8 7 6 5 4 3 2 1

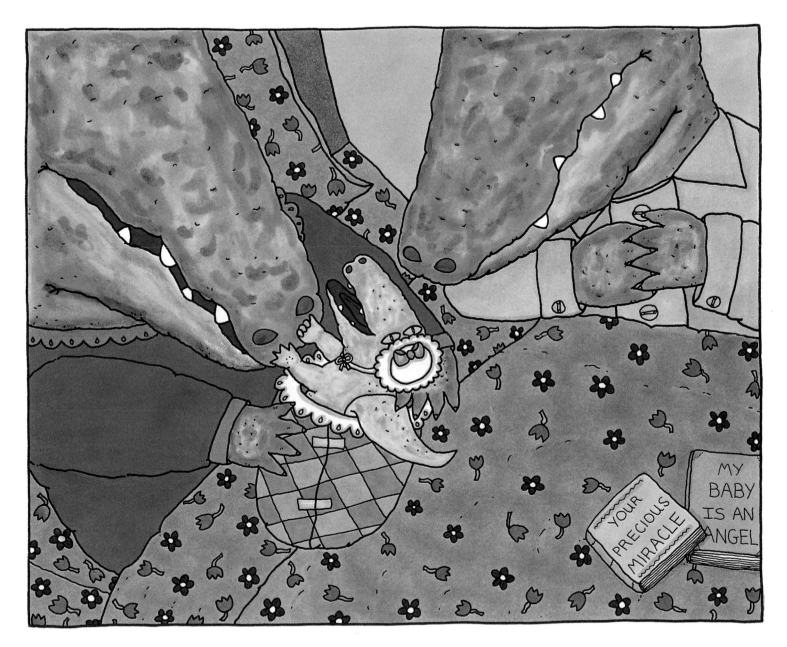

One day, not so long ago, a baby crocodile was born.

The very first thing he did was to bang on his mother's nose.

"Our baby has a lot of energy," the proud parents said.

As he grew older he banged on everything he could reach.

"I hope he grows out of it," said his sister.

But Grandmother said, "That boy has rhythm!" and gave him a drum.

He banged on his drum every day. "Please play outside," said Father.

He banged on his drum every night. "Go to sleep," Mother begged.

He banged on his drum everywhere.

"No more, thank you," his neighbors said politely.

He tried out for school band. "We already have enough drummers," said Mr. Melody.

No one wanted him to bang his drum. But Grandmother said, "Play louder!"

His mother couldn't stand it. His father wouldn't listen. "Quiet!" yelled his sister.

He sadly took his drum into the bathroom. "No more!" they all cried at once.

15

The next day he banged his drum on the subway. People panicked.

Then he went to the library. Nice Mrs. Goodwin yelled, "Get out!"

He went to the park. "Bam, bam," went his drum and a running race began.

He banged his drum at a wedding. The bride cried. The groom dropped the ring.

A parade went by. He banged his drum as hard as he could.

The marchers got out of step and bumped into each other.

The sad crocodile picked up his drum and walked away.

He walked and walked until he was very tired.

He sat down in a deserted alley behind a tall building. Inside, the Boppity Be-Bops were scheduled to perform for the annual animal disco.

Sticks Snarely, the drummer, had not shown up. Marla, the lead singer,
feared that this tardy cat had once again given in to his vice for catnip.

The exhausted crocodile could barely bang on his drum.

Marla opened the door and saw the young crocodile. "We need a drummer fast!" she said.

The band started to play. The crocodile pounded his drum.

The audience went wild!

Just by chance, Harry Hollywood was looking for new talent that night.

"What a beat!" he said. "That crocodile sure knows how to bang a drum."

The happy crocodile pounded his drum louder than ever. Marla sang her heart out. The rest of the band performed as they never had before.

And that night, not so long ago, "Conga Crocodile of the Boppity
Be-Bops" was born.

That was ten gold records ago. Now Conga lives in Los Angeles, where he still bangs his drum and endorses headache relief commercials.